After the CLOTILDA

Africatown's Hidden History

by Anitra Butler-Ngugi

CAPSTONE EDITIONS
a capstone imprint

Published by Capstone Press, an imprint of Capstone
1710 Roe Crest Drive, North Mankato, Minnesota 56003
capstonepub.com

Library of Congress Cataloging-in-Publication Data is available on the Library of Congress website.

ISBN: 9781669074779 (hardcover)
ISBN: 9781669074786 (paperback)
ISBN: 9781669074793 (ebook PDF)

Summary: In 1860, 110 Africans were illegally brought to Mobile, Alabama, aboard the *Clotilda* to be enslaved. After slavery ended in the United States and they gained their freedom, they built their own community in the area—Africatown. For more than 150 years, the people of Africatown have preserved their unique history and culture—and fought for their hard-won community. Learn about the survivors of the *Clotilda*, the community they built, and the people's resilience in the face of encroachment and environmental racism.

Editorial Credits
Editor: Ericka Smith; Designer: Sarah Bennett; Media Researcher: Svetlana Zhurkin; Production Specialist: Katy LaVigne

Image Credits
Alabama Department of Archives and History: 23, 24, Donated by Alabama Media Group/Mobile Press-Register/Photo by Dave Hamby, 26 (bottom); Alamy: Cloudybright/Carmen K. Sisson, 5, 21, Pictorial Press Ltd, 16; Associated Press: Alabama Historical Commission/Daniel Fiore, 28, File/Julie Bennett, 29 (bottom), Jay Reeves, 14, Steve Helber, 25; Getty Images: Bettmann, 8; Library of Congress: 12, 13; Mike Kittrell: 29 (top); The New York Public Library: Schomburg Center for Research in Black Culture/Jean Blackwell Hutson Research and Reference Division, 6, 7, 9, 10 (top); Shutterstock Premier: EPA-EFE/Dan Anderson, cover (top right), 4; Shutterstock: Aastels, 15 (front), George Dodd III, 26 (top), javarman (grunge map), 4 (back) and throughout, Peangdao (water background), cover, 15, Peter Hermes Furian, 10 (bottom), SNicky (brush strokes), cover and throughout, Vitalii1 (texture), cover and throughout; SuperStock: Mary Evans Picture Library, 11, World History Archive/Image Asset Management, 19; U.S. Army Corps of Engineers (map): cover, 1, 17; University of South Alabama: The Doy Leale McCall Rare Book and Manuscript Library/Erik Overbey Collection, 20

Consultant Credits
Dr. Kern Jackson

Printed and bound in China. 5834

Table of Contents

No Way Home

The *Clotilda*

In 1860, 110 African men, women, and children had been captured by people from the Dahomey kingdom (now part of modern-day Benin) and sold to an American. They were forced aboard a ship named the *Clotilda* at the port city of Ouidah and taken thousands of miles away from their home. After a long, torturous trip across the Atlantic Ocean, they were **smuggled** into Mobile, Alabama, to be enslaved—more than 50 years after the **transatlantic slave trade** had been banned in the United States.

The 110 Africans on that ship would become the last known group of Africans brought to the United States to be enslaved. And for five years, they suffered the brutality of slavery. When the Civil War (1861–1865) ended the practice and they regained their freedom, they wanted to go back to the homes they had not forgotten. But that was impossible.

With no way to get back to West Africa, a group of the Africans decided to create their own community in the Mobile area. It would eventually become known as Africatown.

This is the story of their survival, the community they built in Africatown, and the resilience of the people who call Africatown home.

Captured and Sold at Ouidah

The 110 Africans

The Africans held captive in Ouidah who ended up on the *Clotilda* came from many groups, including the Yoruba, the Hausa, the Atakora, and the Nupe. These groups lived on land that is now called Nigeria and Benin. They spoke different languages and practiced different religions. Some had lost their families and friends. Others were captured with their loved ones.

Kossola around 1914

One of the people who would end up on the *Clotilda* was a 19-year-old Yoruba man named Kossola (later called Cudjo Lewis). Kossola enjoyed climbing trees, playing the drums, and playing with his siblings. He had trained as a soldier at the age of 14, and he joined *oro*, a secret society for young men that punished criminals and brought justice to the people in the village. When Dahomeans took Kossola during a raid, he was preparing for marriage.

Another captive was a woman named Ar-Zuma (later called Zuma Livingstone). She was about 23 years old. Historians believe Ar-Zuma was likely Nupe. She was probably Muslim and knew Arabic. And she was likely a wife and a mother when she was captured. By the time she ended up on the *Clotilda*, she had already been sold twice.

Ar-Zuma around 1914

A man named Gumpa (later called Peter Lee) had a more unusual story. Gumpa was from the Dahomey kingdom. He may have been distantly related to the Dahomean king at the time, King Glèlè. Dahomeans did not usually sell their own people into slavery. Historians believe it's possible the Dahomeans gave Gumpa to the American because he was someone King Glèlè did not want around.

A two-year-old girl was also aboard the *Clotilda*. She would later take the name Matilda McCrear. Historians think she was Yoruba. Her mother Gracie and her three sisters were on the *Clotilda* too. McCrear would become the last survivor of the *Clotilda*. When she died in 1940, she was about 82 years old.

A drawing of the Yoruba around 1900

What Were Their Names?

Although the *Clotilda* survivors were forced to take on American names, many still held tightly to their West African names. Sometimes they took Americanized names that were similar to their original names. These are a few of the original and American names historian Sylviane A. Diouf recorded:

African Name	American Name
Abache	Clara Turner
Abila/Abile	Celia Lewis
Adissa	Ardassa Brunston
Ar-Zuma	Zuma Livingstone
Gumpa	Peter Lee
Jaba/Jabi/Jabar	Jaybee/Jaba Shade
Kanko/Kêhounco	Lottie Dennison
Kazoola/Kossola	Cudjo Lewis
Monabee/Omolabi	Katie Cooper
Oloulay/Oluale	Charlie Lewis
Oroh/Wouro	John Auro
Pollee/Kupollee	Pollee Allen
Shamba	Shamba Wigfall

Abache (left) and Kossola
in 1914

The Illegal Slave Trade in Dahomey

King Ghezo (left) of Dahomey

In 1860, the Dahomey kingdom (part of modern-day Benin) was making large sums of money from the slave trade. Several years earlier, King Ghezo of Dahomey had signed a treaty with the British, promising to stop **exporting** captives. Instead, they planned to sell more palm oil. The agreement didn't last. Palm oil did not make as much money as the slave trade. So exporting captives became an important business again.

Even though many countries had banned the international slave trade by 1860, there was still an active illegal slave market. This was partly because there was a huge demand for enslaved people in Cuba. But Africans were smuggled into other countries as well, including the United States.

Through kidnapping, war, and slave raids, Dahomeans captured people from other communities to sell into slavery, including the 110 Africans who ended up on the *Clotilda*. Fishermen, farmers, traders, and people of different religious backgrounds became their victims. These innocent men, women, and children were placed in prisons called *barracoons* after their capture. They were kept there for weeks or even months before being sold into slavery, often from the port city of Ouidah.

A barracoon in West Africa

CHAPTER TWO

Smuggled into Mobile

The Illegal Slave Trade in the United States

Across the Atlantic in the United States, there was also an active illegal slave trade. The transatlantic slave trade had been **outlawed** on January 1, 1808. But the government did little to enforce the ban. In fact, many U.S. presidents actually **pardoned slavers**—people who bought Africans and sold them into slavery—for their crime. And even when Africans were brought in illegally, some states still allowed selling them into slavery.

The *Wanderer* was an American yacht used in the illegal slave trade in the late 1850s.

For enslavers and slavers, smuggling in Africans had an obvious appeal. Cotton was a huge export for the country in the 1800s. So the demand for labor to produce it was great. But the domestic slave trade—buying and selling people already in the United States—was expensive. Smuggled Africans were cheaper for enslavers to purchase. And since being punished for the crime was unlikely, slavers took the risk to buy people cheaply in West Africa and sell them at a huge profit.

The illegal slave trade was profitable in other ways too—especially in New York City. Many slavers left for Africa from New York City's port. Americans provided ships for slavers in other countries. And they helped countries like Brazil and Cuba smuggle in Africans.

By the late 1850s, some Southerners began **advocating** for reopening the international slave trade. Some Northerners condemned this idea—they didn't want slavery to expand, even though some people in the North also played a key role in the illegal trade. Tensions like this around slavery moved the country closer and closer to civil war.

FACT: Until the 1850s, it was largely the British who tried to stop slavers from smuggling Africans across the Atlantic Ocean. The United States did not allow the British to inspect its ships, so American ships could more easily smuggle Africans out of West Africa and into the Americas.

The HMS *Pluto*, a British ship, capturing a large slave ship in 1859

A Well-Planned Crime

Timothy Meaher was a wealthy slaveholder and businessman in Alabama. He was eager to **defy** the government in support of the institution of slavery. He was also confident he could get away with the crime. In 1859, he decided to smuggle in Africans to enslave.

Meaher hired his friend Captain William Foster to make the trip. And he paid $35,000 to use Foster's ship, the *Clotilda*. He also gave Foster $9,000 in gold to purchase people in Ouidah.

Timothy Meaher in 1886

On paper, the *Clotilda* was supposed to bring lumber to the island of St. Thomas. But the real plan was to purchase Africans from West Africa. Foster hired 11 crew members for the trip. They had no idea what their true task was when they left Mobile.

Around March 4, 1860, Foster sailed out of Mobile Bay. During this part of the voyage, the ship got off track, windy weather damaged the ship, and, according to Foster, he had to flee Portuguese ships that were looking for slavers.

After about a 40-day journey, the *Clotilda* arrived at the Cape Verde islands. They repaired the ship. But the crew realized why they'd really been hired and **mutinied**, demanding higher pay. Foster agreed, and they continued on to Dahomey.

A two-masted schooner similar to the *Clotilda*

FACT: The *Clotilda* was an 86-foot (26-meter) schooner with two masts. Captain William Foster built it in 1855 for trading. It was fast and agile, and it had a deep hull that could be used to smuggle people into the country.

Small boats bringing captive Africans to a slave ship
off the west coast of Africa in the 1850s

On May 15, 1860, the *Clotilda* arrived in Ouidah. A little more than a week later, Foster purchased 125 African prisoners. As the prisoners were being ferried to the *Clotilda* in smaller boats, crew members noticed a ship they thought was trying to capture them. Only 110 Africans made it aboard before the *Clotilda* hurriedly set sail.

It took Foster about six weeks to sail from the **Bight** of Benin to the Gulf Coast, a brutal experience for his African victims. The captives were not allowed on deck until the *Clotilda* was far away from ships patrolling West Africa for slavers. Many people became seasick. They had bruises and wounds from the chains placed on them. And they were given little to eat or drink.

The *Clotilda* arrived in the Mississippi Sound around July 8, 1860. A tugboat pulled the ship up the Mobile River. The smuggled captives were moved to a steamboat that brought them to the swamps, where they were hidden for almost two weeks. Then, they were moved to the plantation of Burns Meaher, Timothy Meaher's brother.

To cover up their crime, Foster sailed the *Clotilda* farther up the bay, near Twelvemile Island. Then he set the *Clotilda* on fire and let it sink.

Twelvemile Island, where Foster sank the *Clotilda*

CHAPTER THREE

Five Years of Bondage

Most of the Africans were divided up among enslavers in the Mobile area. Timothy Meaher enslaved 32 people. Burns Meaher enslaved about 20 people. James Meaher, who was also Timothy's brother, enslaved 8 people. And Thomas Buford enslaved about 6 people. Foster enslaved between 5 and 8 Africans. Slave dealers purchased about 24 Africans.

From 1860 until 1865, the *Clotilda* Africans worked under harsh and humiliating conditions as enslaved people. Some of the men enslaved by Timothy Meaher worked in the cotton fields. Others worked on Meaher's steamboats. They transported the cotton to factories. The women cooked, cleaned, and gardened.

But it was clear that the *Clotilda* Africans were different from other enslaved people. Some had facial scars or filed teeth. It was traditional for some groups in West Africa to receive markings or have their teeth filed during certain stages of life. The Africans did not know English, and they were not used to American farming tools. Many of the other enslaved people laughed at them.

The Africans also engaged in acts of resistance. Since they didn't understand the system of enslavement, they defended themselves from beatings and punishment. Once, when an overseer on Burns's plantation tried to whip an African woman working in the fields, a group of the Africans came to her rescue. They grabbed the overseer and whipped him. The overseer didn't whip another African woman after this incident.

Enslaved people loading cotton aboard a steamboat

FACT: Not all of the *Clotilda* survivors ended up in the Mobile area. Some ended up in other parts of Alabama. McCrear was sold to an enslaver who lived in the Tuscaloosa area, and a woman named Redoshi (later called Sally Smith) was sold to an enslaver in the Selma area.

CHAPTER FOUR

An African Town

In 1865, when the Civil War ended, the Africans were happy to regain their freedom. They wanted to go home to West Africa. But they did not have enough money for the trip. And none of them wanted to go back without the others. A group in Mobile decided to settle in the area. They built their own community, using the idea of **collectivism** that they'd learned at home in West Africa.

The Africans organized themselves into a small community and selected a leader. They chose Gumpa (Peter Lee). They also chose Kossola (Cudjo Lewis) to ask Timothy Meaher for land. Meaher had, after all, been responsible for their enslavement and had benefited from their labor. But Meaher refused.

Kossola in his cabin in the 1930s

So the Africans worked and saved their money to purchase land together. In 1870, the *Clotilda* survivors, along with some Alabama-born Black people, purchased seven acres (2.8 hectares) of land from the **estate** of Thomas Buford, one of their former enslavers. They paid $200. This became Lewis Quarters. In 1872, they purchased six more acres (2.4 ha) of land, including four acres (1.6 ha) from the Meahers. This would become Plateau.

The Africans worked together to build one another's homes. Each home was a wooden cabin with a brick chimney. In 1872, they also built a church, Old Landmark Baptist Church (later Union Missionary Baptist Church). And in 1876, they built a graveyard, Old Plateau Cemetery.

Union Missionary Baptist Church in 2022

FACT: The original community the Africans built and its expansion, now called Africatown, includes several neighborhoods—Lewis Quarters, Plateau, Magazine Point, Happy Hills, and Kelly Hills.

To stay connected to their African homes, the town's residents held meetings every Sunday after church. They shared memories of relatives, friends, and food from their previous lives. They raised their children with African traditions. And they taught their children to be charitable and kind to one another.

The Africans also came up with their own way to govern their community and rules to follow. Two men, Jaba and Ossa Keeby, served as judges for the community. If there was a conflict between residents, the community would meet in the evenings to hear all sides.

Although the Africans wanted their children to maintain their native languages, the leaders of the community realized it was important to teach their children the English language and American culture. They built a school and hired a Black teacher to teach their children how to read and write in English.

The community thrived. The women grew fruits and vegetables on the land. Then they sold their produce at the market. The men worked at the railroad yards and the lumber mill.

The Africans had built their community in an isolated part of Mobile, and the second generation of Africatown residents worked together just like their parents had. By the 1920s, the community was the fourth-largest Black town in the country. It was home to approximately 1,500 people.

At first, isolation helped the community thrive on its own terms. But that would change.

Students and their principal (center front) at Mobile County Training
School in Africatown in 1921

Back row, left to right: Alex Reid Jr., Georgia Wymon, Evelyn McCall,
Hattie Keeby, and S.L. Bradley Jr. Front row, left to right: Flora Hauze, Iona
Adams, I.J. Whitley, Lola Brown, and Agnes Finley.

Fighting for Home

As Alabama's economy grew in the 1930s, business shifted from agriculture to industries. This impacted Africatown too.

The *Clotilda* survivors had purchased land from their former enslavers, so the community was tucked inside of what had been the Meaher plantation. In 1929, International Paper Company opened a factory near Africatown on land purchased from the Meahers. In 1940, Scott Paper Company built a factory there too, on land leased from the Meaher family.

Gulf Lumber built a sawmill near Lewis Quarters. And Haas-Davis Packing Company opened a plant for processing meat in the area.

Scott Paper Company's mill in Mobile, Alabama, around the 1950s

New jobs brought new people. Black people moved to the area to work in the factories. By the 1960s, the population in Africatown had grown to more than 10,000 people.

But the new industries also brought environmental pollution to Africatown. Over time, Africatown went from being a community with gardens, fishing, and farming to a community with towering smokestacks and soot-filled air.

Starting in the 1970s, to help stop the **encroachment**, Africatown residents tried to get the community protected as a historical place. Henry C. Williams did much of this work, with little success.

Environmental Racism in the United States

In the United States, some Black neighborhoods have a high number of toxic waste facilities, garbage dumps, and other sources of environmental pollution. This happens because the rules about where to place businesses are not always fair. There are many communities like Africatown:

Louisiana's "Cancer Alley": Oil and gas plants were placed in majority-Black areas, causing an elevated rate of cancer in those communities.

Turkey Creek, Mississippi: This Black community was created by freedpeople in the late 1860s. New developments in the area, including an airport and hotels, damaged the forest and wetlands and polluted the water. This has caused flooding problems for the neighborhood.

Warren County, North Carolina: In the 1980s, a hazardous waste landfill was created next to a Black community in this county.

Protestors in Warren County, North Carolina, in 1982

The new Cochrane-Africatown USA Bridge across the Mobile River

In the 1980s, the state was making plans to replace the old Cochrane Bridge, which would destroy historic homes and the business district in Africatown. Residents fought against construction of the new bridge but lost.

In 2008, a trucking company wanted to build its headquarters in Africatown. This would have created noise and air pollution and damaged the roads. The residents were able to stop it.

People in Africatown in the 1980s

In 2010, oil and gas companies wanted to place new oil-storage tanks in Africatown. This was risky. If the tanks were damaged, the community's drinking water could be polluted.

Africatown was already feeling the negative impact of many manufacturers in town. A lot of residents were sick, and others had died from cancer they believed was caused by the pollution in the area. And Africatown was almost **deserted**. So they mounted a fight against the storage tanks.

In 2013, the residents of Africatown started the Mobile Environmental Justice Action Coalition (MEJAC). In 2015, MEJAC succeeded in helping to keep the new oil-storage tanks out of their community.

In 2017, the residents sued the International Paper Company for damage to their health and to the environment. They claimed that its paper mill released cancer-causing chemicals into the air, ground, and water. The company agreed to a settlement.

Still, there was more work to do. Some Africatown residents believed that locating the sunken *Clotilda* could help. Africatown would have more protection as a historical site, and tourism would help the economy. They started talking with the National Park Service and the Smithsonian Institution about finding the ship.

A Different Future for Africatown?

In January 2018, there was an announcement that Ben Raines, a journalist, might have found the *Clotilda*. But it wasn't the right ship. Not long after, Raines and a team from the University of Southern Mississippi located another ship they believed to be the *Clotilda*. A long review process took place to confirm.

On May 22, 2019, news that the *Clotilda* had been found was released.

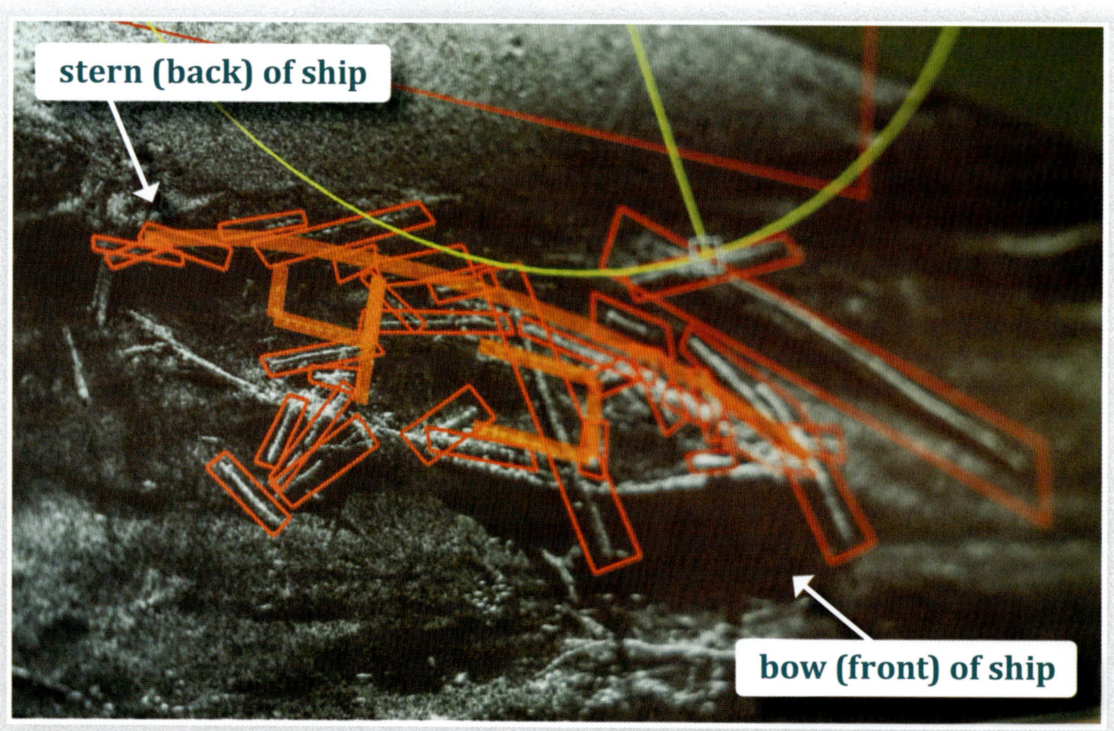

A scanned image of the sunken *Clotilda* in 2022

A celebration in Africatown in 2019

Joycelyn Davis, a descendant of Oluale (Charlie Lewis), was at the press conference announcing the news. As she listened, she thought about how it must have felt to be held captive aboard the ship. Davis was happy that the shipwreck had been found. But she hoped that the news about the ship's discovery would remain focused on the people—and making the conditions better for the families of Africatown.

Since the ship has been located, Africatown has gained more attention for its historical significance. But what that will do for the people of Africatown is not clear yet.

What is clear is that the survivors of the *Clotilda* and their descendants have built an unbreakable community. And they remain determined to protect their home.

FACT: Joycelyn Davis is one of many Africatown residents working to preserve the community's culture. Since 2019, she has organized the Spirit of Our Ancestors Festival to celebrate the 110 Africans who were smuggled into the United States aboard the *Clotilda*.

Glossary

advocate (AD-vuh-kayt)—to support an idea or plan

bight (BITE)—a bay created by a bend in a coastline

collectivism (kuh-LEK-tih-viz-uhm)—a focus on the group rather than the individual

defy (dih-FAHY)—to openly challenge or resist

deserted (dih-ZUHRT-ihd)—empty of people

encroachment (en-KROCH-muhnt)—a gradual takeover of land

estate (ih-STAYT)—a deceased person's property or money

export (ik-SPORT)—to send and sell goods to other countries

mutiny (MYOOT-uh-nee)—a revolt against the captain of a ship

outlaw (OUT-law)—to make something illegal

pardon (PAHR-duhn)—official forgiveness for a serious offense

slaver (SLAY-vuhr)—a person who buys and sells enslaved people

smuggle (SMUHG-uhl)—to bring something or someone into or out of a country illegally

translatlantic slave trade (trans-uht-LAN-tik SLAYV TRAYD)—the movement of millions of Africans across the Atlantic Ocean to be enslaved in North and South America from the 1500s to 1800s

Selected Bibliography

Delgado, James P., Deborah E. Marx, Kyle Lent, Joseph Grinnan, and Alexander DeCaro. Clotilda: *The History and Archaeology of the Last Slave Ship*. Tuscaloosa, AL: University of Alabama Press, 2023.

Diouf, Sylviane A. *Dreams of Africa in Alabama: The Slave Ship* Clotilda *and the Story of the Last Africans Brought to America*. New York: Oxford University Press, 2007.

Newcastle University Press Office. "The Remarkable Life of Matilda McCrear: The Hidden Story of the Last Transatlantic Slave Trade Survivor." *Newcastle University*, March 25, 2020. https://www.ncl.ac.uk/press/articles/archive/2020/03/matildamccrear/.

Raines, Ben. *The Last Slave Ship: The True Story of How* Clotilda *Was Found, Her Descendants, and an Extraordinary Reckoning*. New York: Simon & Schuster, 2022.

Tabor, Nick. *Africatown: America's Last Slave Ship and the Community It Created*. New York: St. Martin's Press, 2023.

Tabor, Nick. "Tar Sands in Africatown: Mobile Environmental Justice Action Coalition." In *The World We Need: Stories and Lessons from America's Unsung Environmental Movement*, edited by Audrea Lim, 4–13. New York: The New Press, 2021.

Index

About the Author

Anitra Butler-Ngugi is a reading specialist and teacher educator who lives in Maryland and Kenya. She teaches children in kindergarten through sixth grade to love reading and to appreciate the English language. She teaches teachers how to design engaging learning experiences for their students. She earned her bachelor's degree and her master's degree from Bowie State University. She enjoys cooking for her husband, traveling, reading, podcasting, and writing books for children.